The Old Ladies Who Liked Cats

By Carol Greene   Pictures By Loretta Krupinski

HarperCollins*Publishers*

for Derron Geuder
—C.G.

The Old Ladies Who Liked Cats
Text copyright © 1991 by Carol Greene
Illustrations copyright © 1991 by Loretta Krupinski
Printed in Mexico. All rights reserved.
Typography by Andrew J. Rhodes

Library of Congress Cataloging-in-Publication Data
Greene, Carol.
    The old ladies who liked cats / by Carol Greene ; pictures by
Loretta Krupinski.
    p.   cm.
    Summary: When the old ladies are no longer allowed to let
their cats out at night, the delicate balance of their island ecology
is disturbed with disastrous results.
    ISBN 0-06-022104-6. — ISBN 0-06-022105-4 (lib. bdg.)
    ISBN 0-06-443354-4 (pbk.)
    [1. Ecology—Fiction.]   I. Krupinski, Loretta, ill.   II. Title.
PZ7.G82845Ol   1991   90-4443
[E]—dc20   CIP
                                                        AC

The illustrations in this book were painted on three-ply
Strathmore Bristol board in gouache with color pencils.

Note

For many years, scientists have known that plants and animals need each other. Each has a particular job in its community. If that job isn't done, the whole community can fall apart.

To show this mutual need among creatures, Charles Darwin told a story about clover and cats. Other scientists added their own thoughts and observations until the story became almost an ecological folktale.

In this version of the tale, I've made a number of changes. But I've kept the main idea, because like the main idea of most folktales, it is true.

—C.G.

Once there was an island with a town in the center,

and beyond the town grew fields of sweet red clover,

and beyond the fields stretched a dark green forest,
all the way to the sea,

and on the sea sailed the navy, round and round the island, keeping it safe.

Now, the sailors in the navy were strong and healthy because they drank plenty of good fresh milk that came from the cows in the fields,

and the cows gave the good fresh milk
because they ate plenty of sweet red clover,

and the clover grew thick
because long-tongued bees carried pollen from blossom to blossom,

and the bees carried pollen
because there were no field mice to eat their honeycombs,

and there were no field mice
because cats from town chased them into the forest,

and the cats chased the mice because the old ladies who liked cats let them out each night and said, "Chase those mice and keep our island safe!" (They were wise old ladies, you see, and knew how things work together.)

But late one night, the mayor of the town went for a
walk, tripped over a cat, and fell flat on his face in a puddle.
"I shall make a new law!" he cried. "From now on, cats
must stay inside at night. That will keep our island safe."

The old ladies who liked cats sighed and shook their heads,
but they kept their cats inside at night,

and the cats couldn't chase the field mice,
and the field mice ate the honeycombs,

and the long-tongued bees stopped carrying pollen,

and the clover grew thin and sour,

and the cows gave poor milk,

and the sailors became weak and sickly,

and one night invaders came.

They sailed right past the navy, swarmed through the forest, trampled over the fields, stomped into the town, and shouted, "This is our island now!"

In the days that followed, they ate everything in sight, littered the streets, frightened the children, and took up all the room.

"What shall we do?" cried the townsfolk.

"What shall we do?" cried the mayor.

"This is what you must do," said the old ladies who liked cats. (They were wise old ladies, you'll remember, and knew how things work together.) "You must change your law and let our cats out at night. Then the island will be safe again."

The mayor scratched his head. "Imagine that!" he said. "All right. The law is changed."

So out came the cats that chased the field mice,

and away ran the mice and left the honeycombs,

and back came the long-tongued bees that carried the pollen,

and up grew the clover, thick and sweet,

and the cows ate plenty and gave good fresh milk,

and the sailors drank plenty and became strong and healthy,

and one day they threw the invaders off the island.

"Well done!" said the mayor, and pinned medals on them all.

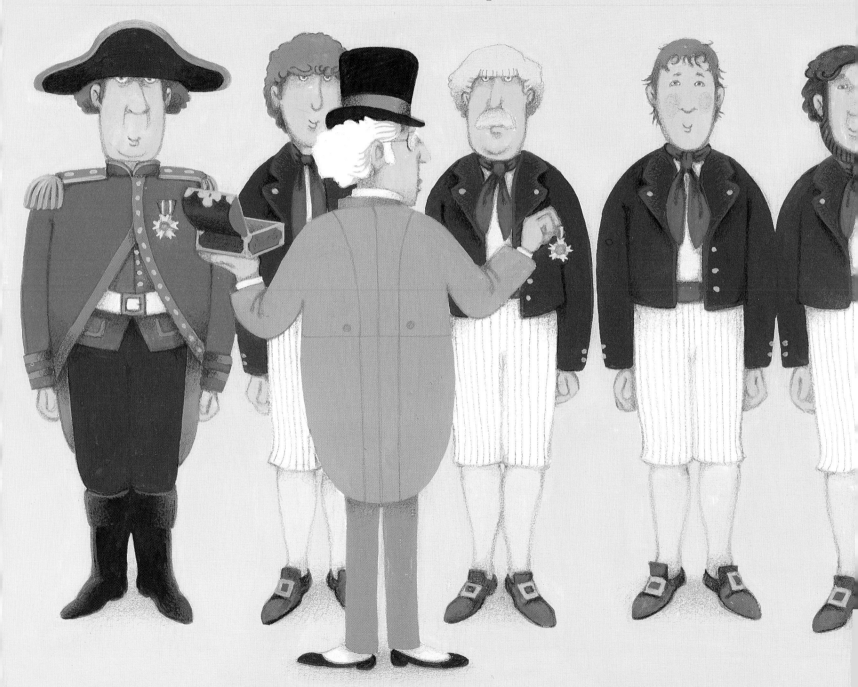

But the sailors took them off and gave them to the real heroes…

the old ladies who liked cats.